Dear Parent:

Congratulations! Your child is taking the first steps on an exciting journey. The destination? Independent reading!

STEP INTO READING® will help your child get there. The program offers five steps to reading success. Each step includes fun stories and colorful art. There are also Step into Reading Sticker Books, Step into Reading Math Readers, Step into Reading Write-In Readers, Step into Reading Phonics Readers, and Step into Reading Phonics First Steps! Boxed Sets—a complete literacy program with something for every child.

Learning to Read, Step by Step!

Ready to Read   Preschool–Kindergarten
• big type and easy words • rhyme and rhythm • picture clues
For children who know the alphabet and are eager to begin reading.

Reading with Help   Preschool–Grade 1
• basic vocabulary • short sentences • simple stories
For children who recognize familiar words and sound out new words with help.

Reading on Your Own   Grades 1–3
• engaging characters • easy-to-follow plots • popular topics
For children who are ready to read on their own.

Reading Paragraphs   Grades 2–3
• challenging vocabulary • short paragraphs • exciting stories
For newly independent readers who read simple sentences with confidence.

Ready for Chapters   Grades 2–4
• chapters • longer paragraphs • full-color art
For children who want to take the plunge into chapter books but still like colorful pictures.

STEP INTO READING® is designed to give every child a successful reading experience. The grade levels are only guides. Children can progress through the steps at their own speed, developing confidence in their reading, no matter what their grade.

Remember, a lifetime love of reading starts with a single step!

For Mom and Dad
—K.D.

Step into Reading, Random House, and the Random House colophon are registered trademarks
of Random House, Inc.

Visit us on the Web!
www.stepintoreading.com

Educators and librarians, for a variety of teaching tools, visit us at
www.randomhouse.com/teachers

Library of Congress Cataloging-in-Publication Data
Depken, Kristen L.
Rudolph the red-nosed reindeer / adapted by Kristen L. Depken;
illustrated by Linda Karl. — 1st ed.
p. cm.
ISBN 978-0-375-86202-1 (trade) — ISBN 978-0-375-96202-8 (lib. bdg.)
I. Karl, Linda. II. Rudolph the Red-Nosed Reindeer (Television program) III. Title.
PZ7.D4396Ru 2009 [E]—dc22 2009005738

Printed in the United States of America   10 9 8 7 6 5 4 3 2 1

RUDOLPH
THE
RED-NOSED REINDEER®

Adapted by Kristen L. Depken
Cover illustrated by Artful Doodlers Ltd.
Interior illustrated by Linda Karl

Random House 🏠 New York

Santa and his elves
lived in Christmastown.
They made toys
all year long.

One day,

a reindeer was born.

His name was Rudolph.

He had a red nose.

It glowed!

His parents were worried.

Rudolph's father

hid Rudolph's nose.

All the reindeer
wanted to pull
Santa's sled.
They were learning to fly.
Rudolph joined them.

Rudolph met Clarice.

She liked Rudolph.

Rudolph flew in the air!

The reindeer
cheered for Rudolph.
He was happy.

Rudolph's
fake nose fell off.
The reindeer laughed.
They called him Rudolph
the Red-Nosed Reindeer.

Poor Rudolph!

He ran away.

Hermey the elf
ran away, too.
He did not want
to make toys.
He wanted to be
a dentist.

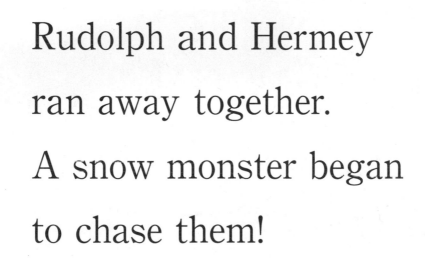

Rudolph and Hermey
ran away together.
A snow monster began
to chase them!

A man named
Yukon Cornelius
helped them.

Yukon chopped the ice.
They floated away
from the monster.

They floated to an
island filled with toys.
These were toys
no one wanted.

The king of the island
wanted Rudolph to find
homes for the toys.
Rudolph knew
Santa would help.

The snow monster
could see Rudolph's nose.
Rudolph wanted to
protect his friends.

That night,

he left.

Rudolph went home.

His parents and Clarice

were missing!

The snow monster
had them!
Rudolph went
to the monster's cave.

Rudolph saved Clarice.
But the monster
grabbed him!

Yukon and Hermey
found Rudolph
just in time!

Hermey called
the snow monster.
Yukon dropped a rock
on the monster's head!

Everyone was safe!
They all went back
to Christmastown.

It was Christmas Eve!
But there was
a big storm.
Santa would have to
cancel Christmas!

Rudolph's nose
started to glow.
Santa got an idea.

Rudolph's nose
could light the way.

Christmas was saved!
Santa found homes
for all the toys.
And Rudolph
became the most
famous reindeer of all.